GONE

OrangeBooks Publication

Website: www.orangebooks.in

First Edition 2025

ISBN: 978-93-6554-432-9

Price: Rs. 250.00

Printed in India

GONE

Stories on Loss, Heartache, and More

Veeksha Vagmita

OrangeBooks Publication
www.orangebooks.in

For

My dearest Vaibhav, a great brother and a gem of a person

And

My manager, Mr. Mukesh, who is an emblem of what it means to be human.

Your support has helped me beyond description. Souls like you deserve a special place in heaven.

Contents

Preface 1-3

The Discovery of Evil 7-20

Joys and Jolts 21-31

Hope Flies Away 32-45

Gone 46-57

Bumpy Ride on a Starry Night 52-70

Acknowledgements 71-72

Preface

The stories in this collection are reflective and written mostly in the stream-of-consciousness mode. They focus on the action unfolding within the inner world of the characters. The form of the stories is experimental. They delve into the minute workings of the characters' consciousness, bringing to the fore the dramatic life of the mind. Inspired by real-life experiences, the stories seamlessly blend the personal with the fictional. The narratives have a philosophical undertone and contemplate broad themes like loss, love, heartbreak, hatred, and the manner in which difficult experiences become a source of illumination. Despite the untypical nature of the stories and their leisurely musings on varying themes, they should not be interpreted as self-indulgent. I make a conscious departure from the format of short stories to carve brief narratives with a distinctive form. When I began writing these stories, a part of me wanted to avoid the well-trodden path. Despite the creative risk, I wrote narratives exemplifying organicity, relinquishing a conscious design. I let my imagination run freely, unconstrained by the dictates of form or convention.

The stories narrate life-changing events in free-wheeling, flowing prose. They reveal the wisdom gained in hindsight as well as the jolts occasioned by an encounter with evil, whose dailiness and banality are simply a prelude to something far more sinister with a much greater scope. Needless to say, I had Hannah Arendt in mind while dwelling upon the phenomenon of "evil". Facing the hard truths of life, love and human nature acts as a catalyst for evolution.

The title of the story has a deeply personal touch. For many of us, there comes a day in our lives when the person closest to our heart is left only in our heart—a day when our life threatens to fall apart. No matter how deeply we mourn their loss, there's no escaping the painful reality that our loved one is GONE.

And yet, transcending the trappings of mortality, the love we shared with them lives on.

Veeksha Vagmita

Wisdom that isn't distilled in our own crucible can't help us.

— Chitra Banerjee Divakaruni

1

The Discovery of Evil

She always knew the world was cruel, unimaginably cruel, and the incalculable suffering caused by this insane cruelty. And yet, Meena had been naïve enough to never feel the visceral reality of a simple truth flowing from something she already knew: Not everyone was good. Just because she was a creature fashioned to feel intensely for others, it did not therefore follow that everyone experienced life the same way and was likely to respond in a manner that agreed with her. Not everyone had the same mental make-up; not everyone possessed the qualities intrinsic to her nature. Not that there was a dearth of benevolent souls in this bewildering world: a world blighted by the banality of everyday acts of evil: acts perceived as too "commonplace" for alarm or censure. Given the dailiness of minor acts of cruelty, it is natural for most people to become inured to micro aggressions actuated by evil, little knowing that this is not the way of the world but a corruption of human nature, laying the groundwork for far greater atrocities, which turn out to be anything but banal. Once the banal acts of evil devolve into sheer barbarity, their gravity and scale make them dreadfully difficult to contain. It is always the same old story—a repetition of the historical curse of "too little, too late" with the oft-repeated lament "How did we let this happen?" hanging heavy in the air.

Meena knew all this and more but you never truly understand evil until it is standing at your own door. At some point, the reality of evil is bound to hit you in the gut. You have to be God's favourite child to be shielded from this ugly truth, but even that doesn't seem to cut much ice. God tests us all. Some go through a trial by fire. Some lurch from setback to setback. Some walk on air as fortune decides to smile on them, saving them a great deal of struggle that is the lot of others. Some are beset by numerous small challenges that test their mettle and enhance their endurance. And then come those whose existence is one long ordeal: a lifelong test of their patience and resilience. Maybe it's designed to make them stronger. Maybe it's a sinister scheme to trap them in a life resembling a pressure cooker: a life that leaves them burnt and browbeaten. Who can penetrate the motives of this moody and mysterious universe? And who can fully understand the staggering complexity of human nature? Allowing the daily erosion of our collective humanity weakens our moral fibre and warps our intrinsic nature. And it all happens so slowly that we often fail to foresee the long-term consequences of the daily corruption of our humanness. There are *certain* traits that make us truly human. A proclivity to form and further evil designs is *certainly* not one of them.

For most thinking people, the question that holds the greatest significance is "Am I doing the right thing?". These are people who know the meaning of love and set great store by relationships based on care. For the self-aggrandizing souls obsessed with maintaining control, the question that matters is vastly different: "Am I the smartest person in the room whose wish is the command for everyone within view?"

After strategically and cold-heartedly tearing down *presumed* rivals, *potential* rivals, *imagined* rivals, *dreamed-up* rivals and anyone with the distant possibility of somehow becoming a rival, they often manage to establish themselves as smarter than the rest, unrivalled in every respect—a feat accomplished by design and not by talent.

Meena had no idea that people could invest an enormous amount of energy in scheming, plotting, bullying, and many other things that cast them in a poor light besides wasting a good deal of their precious time. When she came face to face with this dark reality, she entertained the idea that those who were not (always) good must have some virtues. There must be some redeeming features in all God's creatures.

Eventually, she learnt how even the souls of decent people were compromised by choice, circumstances, or both. And their inhumanity was the hardest to fathom. They doubtlessly knew better, yet their words and actions screamed otherwise.

The haunting question, "*How did we let this happen?*" was always asked too late. It had been emptied of all meaning, so often had it been repeated to mourn the trail of destruction left by needless aggression.

Strangely enough, when another opportunity presented itself to change course and acquit ourselves honourably for once, history repeated itself and, that too, with a vengeance. We were shown a film we had seen many times before and would have been grateful to never have to watch it anymore. Still, the question presented itself: "How on earth did we let this happen?" The answer was mortifyingly simple: "You let this happen. You know it. And that's it."

This crude reality hit Meena like a lightning bolt when she took a solo trip to Chennai two years ago. She encountered the worst tendencies in human beings on a traumatic night at the beach—a night she had waited for and imagined with great alacrity. She wanted to feel the magic of the sea late at night, knowing full well the risky nature of such an adventure. But her desire to see the undulating waves, and the water glimmering underneath the full moon, got the better of her. She witnessed a lot except it was nothing she had expected or wanted to watch. A young woman lay sprawled on the beach, crying her heart out. But every ten minutes, some decent-looking person would ridicule, shame and taunt her. Some of the taunts were so denigrating—*Oh, let's not poke, disturb and irritate the animal*—that it made Meena's blood boil. Were these people human beings? They kept inflicting emotional injuries on the woman as if it was some enjoyable game. They insulted her with their *obnoxious word-play* and were overweeningly proud of their diabolical creativity. What were they proud of? Their ability to successfully aggravate a wounded person's suffering by saying exactly what would cut her to the bone. They seemed mighty pleased with their murderous concoction of words. The beach was crowded with many regular people who seemed content to be passive onlookers. Or were they secretly deriving sadistic pleasure from this "spectacle" of torture? Were they vicariously living out their pathological fantasies? They kept a straight face and never opened their mouths. Their passivity was complicity. Silent spectators of this gory pastime couldn't absolve themselves of the guilt of failing to intervene. It was clear that they didn't care to intervene. But what troubled Meena was the feeling that they probably didn't *want* to intervene. Either they were dumb, spineless or just a shade better than their monstrous peers.

The woman being targeted must have possessed uncommon reserves of strength because she had been at the receiving end of gratuitous violence for a few years now. Meena wondered why the woman even stepped out of her house in such a hostile atmosphere. It was only a year later that the answer came to her in the voice of the persecuted woman, "Because I wanted to live in freedom. I couldn't imprison myself because some arbitrary tyrants decided to make my life hell. Without freedom, there is no life. And living in fear is worse than not living at all."

So, the young woman would choose to move around with her head held high.

Meena saw her walking to the marketplace. The woman walked a little unsteadily and was wiping tears from her eyes. Attacking this woman, who was probably one among many, had been turned into a sport played for the sadistic enjoyment of the tourists. From a wholesome place that attracted tourists on a vacation, the beach had been turned into a site of torture. Mean jokes were cracked by seemingly decent men and women, adding new layers of injury to the wounds inflicted on blameless souls.

Infuriated, Meena waylaid a girl who presented herself as soft-spoken and genial but followed the command to direct covert jibes at suffering souls without protest and perhaps without remorse. Meena told her that disguised violence was no less hurtful than a direct attack. In fact, a direct attack could be fought off but disguised violence couldn't be tackled directly. "Why do you do this? You act sweet but your actions bely that sweetness. What are you trying to be? A loyal soldier to corrupt masters? Don't you have a mind of your own? And where is your heart? Superficial sweetness will not absolve you of the pain you have caused by your seemingly innocuous, but actually vicious, words, even if they were not your own. You wounded someone and made a grotesque game out of it." The girl lacked the courage to look reality in the eye, so she refused to acknowledge Meena's words and presence.

A few days later, the girl confronted Meena. In a self-righteous manner, she told Meena to learn to be more polite. All this while, the girl was complicit in the humiliation and ridicule of wounded souls, and yet she had the temerity to ask *Meena to be polite*. This girl could live in a fool's paradise, but those with a conscience would see through her in no time. Somebody needed to tell the girl politely that sneakily enabling abuse was immoral and far more offensive than anything impolite anyone might ever say. It dawned on Meena that once you took the crooked path, your moral compass was lost and you could only mouth inanities. Once you had compromised your conscience, you were never going to retrieve your authentic and humane self. It was no use trying to reason with lost souls; they were lost and might never find themselves. And she didn't want to talk to the diminished and degraded version of what they once were and had now ceased to be.

2

Joys and Jolts

Five years ago, she had no inkling of the disaster that awaited her. She failed to read the signboards on the way. She plodded through the rocky terrain of a complicated love, half-wishing to turn around and return to her comfort zone. But the thirst for a romantic adventure spurred her on. It kept her moving in a direction that didn't feel right in her bones. Soon enough, she hit a dead end. She should have viewed it as "The End". It would have saved her bucketfuls of tears—tears that she cried in vain, utterly in vain.

How she wished she had been less focused! The intense focus that she prided herself on, and that had helped her forge ahead in life, proved counter-productive in this unusual romantic escapade. Had she been a little less focused, a little less earnest, and a little less intent on making progress, she might have seen the blindingly clear writing on the wall. It screamed out that this could only go so far; it would only go so far; it wasn't meant to go any further. Despite having an unerring instinct, which set off alarm bells every time she took a step forward, she couldn't help clinging to her tender hopes—hopes that ensnared her with their illusory charm.

Well, love makes fools of us all. But it may not completely blind us to the reality, especially if we have a mind disciplined enough to not stray too far. She had a mind trained to hold on to clarity even when the warm, fuzzy feeling of romance seemed too inviting to be inspected closely. She also had a heart schooled to make wise choices—a carefully cultivated virtue that offered a safeguard against chasing love that resisted transparency even as it kept up a beguiling façade of unequalled and unwavering ardour. Life has a way of dismantling our defences and catapulting us into undreamed-of situations. It can leave us trapped in a maze that robs us of a sense of direction, leaving us adrift in a world sufficiently chaotic for another layer of lost-ness. The labyrinthian twists and turns narrow our focus to managing our emotions in the current moment. The lost-ness engendered by love washes away apprehensions about the future. We cannot look past immediate occurrences or make new plans to build a life without encumbrances. Love can reduce us to a bundle of emotions by winning us with promises glowing with conviction—promises that can break us as easily they can be broken.

To be fair, it is easy to lose our way in the first stirrings of love: a ridiculously rapturous state that can easily spell trouble. Giddy with foolish excitement, we are transported to another realm—a realm that elevates us above the mundanity of life. Close on the heels of this exhilarating high comes a sharp drop—gravity, full of glee, seizes the opportunity to reassert itself.

Oh, how we mistake the slightest infatuation, the fleeting ecstasy of flesh meeting flesh, for an epic romance or a grand passion. Oh, those Shakespearean romances! They turned people's head the moment they got played on the Elizabethan stage. They hooked the audience so tightly that we've been hooked to them for generations. She fancied herself in a Shakespearean romance and lost all common sense. The red flags passed her by in a procession, but she kept believing her lover was a good person. Either her love is blind or it was too deep for her to emerge from the haze of passion that surrounded her being. Things could go only two ways. Either she pulled herself out of the morass of a toxic romance or let herself get sucked into this miserably mushy mess if she was too besotted to return to her senses.

Well, things couldn't go either way. She struggled hard to extricate herself from the quagmire but she was dragged into it the moment he kindled the hope of a union—a hope she had held so dear that even a sliver of it awakened by eloquent words, throbbing with emotions, would weaken her resolve and get her back into the mushy mess that could never have turned into anything more. By the time she learnt the art of ignoring love-bombing and realize the limitations of hope, her life had change beyond recall, a dagger had pierced my soul, her legs refused to carry her, her strength almost deserted her.

She knew life was hard. She always knew that. But she didn't know how cruel the quirks of fate could be and how much a broken heart could bleed. She didn't know the rhapsodic rapture of love was followed by a daze that robbed everything of clarity: words spoken by a friend or your father slipped through the cracks of your mind. Though she had immense self-control, love can be the undoing of the strongest of souls. Though drifting into a dreamland, she wasn't anxious to break the spell. The ungovernable and irrepressible passion had a vitality that made her feel alive. And she hadn't realized the hope she clung to would be gone in the blink of an eye.

She had fallen in love with a man she held in great esteem. Admiration came instantly, naturally, effortlessly. Sunshine filled the void within. She dabbed powder on her cheeks to hide her deep blush at the mention of his name. She glowed like a newlywed, even though her virginity was firmly intact. He seduced her with words, and she believed he loved her with a passion that equalled hers. It was true but their love was doomed. She thought she had found her resting place. Her small, humble umbrella could shield them from the rain. She could lie in his arms, and he could share his hopes and pain. It was a new beginning to be superseded by a sudden end. The love that felt like a godsend dissolved like a vapour, leaving no trace. All that remained were memories locked in her head. No pictures together, no date to remember, no conversation that broke the barriers. She wished she had known he would treat her so ill that the pain would lessen but remain still. She wasn't good enough for him. Now he's not good enough for her. "You could marry the whole town, and I couldn't care less. I hope one day you see yourself in the mirror and realize how carelessly and cruelly you broke a heart after keeping it in chains in the name of hope that never meant anything. Stay happy but never try to come closer. It's over." He watched her silently. No words of comfort. No apology.

In his reckless haste, he threw away something truly sublime There was so much they had in common. And there was no dearth of time. She liked his mind, his beautiful mind. She drank the words that flowed from his pen. She pored over his musings. They developed their own love language. It was so achingly sweet. Her heart throbbed with delight. This happened only once in a lifetime. (Although it happened again, that love too went down in flames.)

That moment is now gone. The days are dolefully dark. There's nothing to break the silence. Except the thunderbolts. Except the gunshots. Except the beating of a tired heart. How did she get here? How did this happen? Did this happen? Life barely crawls in this blurry, shadowy region—between dream and wakefulness, between hope and despair, between drama and ennui, between *you and me*.

Where is the exit? I must be in a movie hall. My life plays on my mind's screen. I want to be the director, but I'm only a spectator. Jeers and whispers ring in my ears. Some cheer me on; some let me down. God must be here. Or, I wouldn't have survived this long. The show must go on. The show must stop. I scan the faces. He, too, must be here. The one who vowed to stay; the one who slipped away. He is always there. He is never there. When the darkness lifts and the doors open, he may come to me. If I live to see the day.

Why didn't he protect me? He was no swashbuckling hero. No knight in shining armour. No death-defying lover. He was a mere mortal. That was enough. More than enough. But he forgot to be human. He just watched with his eyes wide open. As if I was a mystery. As if he didn't know me. He was soaring in his jet plane. On the top of his game. I've met him so many times … in my dreams, in my reveries, in places I've never seen. Nothing could be more surreal. Nothing could be more real. I was charmed. Smitten. Bewitched. Why couldn't I see my future, written so clearly on the wall? Was it a quest for adventure that took me so far into love? In a land that's unknown, a land I cannot leave. I can neither breathe in freedom, nor die in blessed peace.

3

Hope Flies Away

It started with an email (my old-fashioned heart calls it a 'letter'). Proper and polite. Just the way it should be. The universe looked on; the gods in the heavens yawned. No one could have divined what the Lord had in mind. No love was in the air. Not a flicker of romance anywhere. But the story began. A woman wrote to a man.

Oh, that letter! It would change my life forever. Life had pounced on me before. I had had my share of woes. Having burnt my fingers, I wrote with exquisite care. I slowed my racing mind and steadied my quivering hand. A shadow I couldn't yet see loomed darkly over me. He replied. A man of fine words. Tongue-tied in love but eloquent in the larger world. His words—so gentle, so beguilingly simple—found their way to my heart. That was no small thing since I kept a stronger armour at all times lest something or someone carried me away and blurred my focus on the things that truly mattered to me. It's still a mystery how a few simple words breached an armour strengthened over years. Inside my head, his words pranced around merrily. Undecided about my feelings, I chose to let them be. As it turned out, his words carried more power than I could resist. They were darts shot by Cupid himself, or so it seemed in the first flush of romance. Back then, I knew too little to understand that words, however eloquent and heartfelt, can be no less dangerous than those without the cloak of politeness and subtle tenderness.

Trouble awaited me but I didn't have a clue. I was in my thirties, long past the age when you turn giddy and give yourself away at the slightest hint of a crackling chemistry. I knew the dangers of foolish infatuation; the jolts that followed such thoughtless elation. My romantic errors had taught me a lot. I could dodge Cupid's darts with practised ease. This wasn't really a challenge for me. Or, was it? A feeling stole over me; it had a will stronger than mine. I kept it at arms' length; I fought with every atom of my strength. I knew feelings, however intense and feverish, generally had a lifespan. If you didn't allow them to take over you, they were bound to fade away with time. I had succeeded many times in conquering infatuation in its early stages. You just had to keep your head empty, quell your curiosity, and stay away, online and offline, from the object of your developing feelings. It was a tried-and-tested method, and it simply couldn't fail. As it turned, it did. It did fail, and still can't figure out why. Fate, destiny, the divine hand—something had a role to play. I tried to refrain from engaging with the guy, keeping a stiff exterior till the feeling had passed me by. I had faced strong temptations before. But my steely resolve had seen me through. Did it come to rescue and extricate me from this emotional entanglement. The short answer is no. The long answer is also no. This was something different, and I felt out of my depth.

So, did I win this battle with ever-growing infatuation? I never doubted my capacity for restraint and the strength of my resolve. So, I was in for a shock when I finally lost. And, it didn't feel like a pleasant shock. It simply came as a pure shock.

I still marvel at the intensity of that fever. It was silly and yet sublime. A pretty stranger had invaded my mind. He danced inside my head, laying claim to my affection. I tried to throw him out, but he stayed etched in my brain. Suddenly, my younger self came to the surface. I ordered her to leave, but she wanted to intervene. She knew something that I had forgotten. *Love just happens.* No! No! I couldn't follow her "wise" counsel. I couldn't entertain a vain hope. I had striven hard to discipline my mind. I couldn't lose self-control.

Who can fight love when it comes at you with all its force? It is beautiful. It is tyrannical. It carries you away in spite of yourself. This budding love drove me onward. I wanted to slow down, but couldn't match up to its power. A song played in the background. *Wise men say only fools rush in. But I can't help falling in love with you.* The universe smiled. Or, was it a smirk? It had a plan I could never have guessed. I played the song over and over. It was a balm to my besotted heart. What did I see in those banal letters? Why did they speak to my soul? Why did I even bother? He felt nothing at all. I was sure of that. Well, not so sure. Was there something hidden between the lines? I tried to still my racing mind. I needed to go slow. My heart was entangled with his. No ordinary romance was this.

As we wrapped up our first round of mails, my feelings started to take shape. He seemed to possess the qualities I prized highly. He was thorough, precise, prompt and polite. I looked for his pictures online. There was dignity in his demeanour and depth in his eyes. He was nothing if not sorted and mature. Were we kindred spirits? I wondered. As I roamed this dreamy landscape, the older me clucked in dismay. "Don't judge a man by his picture," she warned. "Marry in haste, repent at leisure," I added (to soothe and silence her). Though I had sense enough to watch my step, I couldn't crush these tender emotions. Nor did I want the safety of shallow flirtation. Love I will if love it really was. I would nurture this bud without coaxing it to bloom. If it held any promise, it would open up on its own and nourish me in return. I just had to pay attention. I just had to give it a chance. That was my biggest fault. I should have waited for a while, and if no love bloomed openly before my eyes, I would have firmly said goodbye.

Fool that I was, I gave this wishy-washy expression of love a chance it simply didn't deserve. It's easy to make statements in retrospect, but it's terribly difficult to show that wisdom in a delicate moment. I didn't give this love a chance. I gave it chance after chance after chance, much to my detriment.

But then, it was in my nature to forgive and lovingly persist. He seemed to be a man with ample sense, deserving of my patience. I sustained myself with radical hope.

Something started to hiss and crackle. A fire ripped through my dream landscape. Who started it? Flames danced before my eyes. Roses turned to ashes; smiles turned to tears.

Before me lay the ruins of my hope. It's something I will always remember.

My heart weeps whenever I look back. It's too much to hold, too much to mourn.

Sometimes I don't even have to look back. The past rises up and sits with me. It will sit with me forever. First there was light. Then flew the sparks. Soon, we were staring at a relentless blaze. Fury fed the growing flames. He watched in horror. I cried in despair. Fire! Fire! Can anyone help? Oh, the baffling complexity of humans! He took all the promises and dashed them to pieces. In the shards of our love was a story untold. In the shards of our love was the sanctity of truth. The truth that cannot be tainted by lies; the truth that transcends the trickery of words; the truth that likes to speak for itself.

Three years ago, he did not know. How the virus of doubt infects a healthy mind; how it enters one's veins and poisons the source of life. He was no match for this sly intruder. It filled his mind with bizarre notions. He shunned what he needed the most: the wisdom of his kind heart. Did the noise drown out his inner voice? Where did the feeling, the music, go?

Who can deny the visceral effect of words? Sights and sounds come wrapped up in them. Love and malice gain force from them. They are bundles of raw energy. His words were like sparkling gems. They lit up the gloomy recesses of my mind. They captured the hushed cries of the heart. When did they turn to rayless stones—without warmth, without light? His thoughtless words cut me to the bone. They were aimed at me with deadly precision. Did a nightmare disrupt my waking life? Or, was I dreaming with eyes wide open?

How did the story take this turn? Did I not sense the approaching storm? I can say 'yes', and I can say 'no'. There are no happy answers when things go wrong. I was wide awake, watching every step, seeing every sign. I sighed over the mess, but I believed too much in my own good sense. I wouldn't submit to a heedless force; I had strength enough to stay my course. I couldn't see clearly the limits of my powers. If he had held my hand, we would have found our way together. But that was a forlorn hope, flimsier than a feather. Even a gust of wind could carry him away; even a whisper could shake his feeble faith. Our ship sank before it could sail; it was more than any heart could take. Everything I shared with him—the dreams, the hopes, the ideas, the jokes—was written on my psyche. The memories we created would follow me around.

Hope renewed as the days passed. It was a feeling that kept me strong. A bulwark against the hissing, harrowing storm. Even before the darkness descended, hope had kept our hearts warm. "We know what our future is going to look like," he had said in his guarded way. The future must be bright. Now that we had found each other. No hope could be more tender than the hope that entwined our hearts. Two years later, he got married to someone else. Did he mourn "our future" when he went through the wedding rituals? He kept the news under wraps for as long as he could. He was trying to hold on to me. Was he holding on to our broken dream? When I learnt the truth, my heart burst with anguish. Death would have hurt less than the sight of our dead future. The music played no more. Hope had flown our dreamy nest.

What kept me chained to this ill-fated romance? Was it the yearning of an aching heart? Or, the tenacity of a traumatic bond? Was it the madness of fiery passion? Or, the tenderness of pure affection? So many questions wrestled inside my head. So much left behind. So much left unsaid. Answers eluded me, just like him. I raised my teary eyes to the heavens above.

The sun shone with innocent delight, marking the end of a care-worn night. "For you, a thousand times over." How I had clung to those magical words! Maybe I missed him.

Maybe I missed love.

4

Gone

He was not there. She picked up the book that had once made them erupt into peals of laughter. They had listened to the audio version of *Master and Margarita* by the Russian author Mikhail Bulgakov a hundred times. It was a masterful, mesmerizing narration of the novel, which stayed in their minds and figured in our conversations for a long time to come. Though Papa was well-versed in Russian literature, this was one masterpiece he hadn't chanced upon. She flattered herself on having introduced him to a book belonging to a realm of literature he was far more familiar with. Even now, now that he was gone, she still hadn't read enough to match up to his knowledge of Russian literature.

Her dad had been a fan of Russian literature and loved to draw lessons from the books he had read in those days when he was young. Oh, it was a golden period when responsibilities hadn't weighed him down and denied him the leisure needed to appreciate fine books.

His fascination with Russian authors went hand in hand with his romance with socialism: a term which seemed to take in its sweep the communist ideology. She was never clear about the differences and overlaps between socialism and communism. They were often used interchangeably, so she wondered if they had been collapsed into one term signifying the same thing. If Papa was still here, she would have asked him to clear this confusion, once and for all. She couldn't help wishing he had stayed a while longer.

In his youth, socialism was the ideology espoused by progressive Indians, many of whom must have been youngsters with raging passions. The idea of a revolution must have been irresistibly charming. She was not certain when Papa got wedded to the socialist ideology, but it seems to be somewhere during the 70s and 80s, culminating in a nasty divorce in the 90s. The excesses of the Far Left had left him profoundly disillusioned. He made it amply clear to fellow members of his socialist outfit that the shadow of the red flag must never fall on him again. Not surprisingly, he invited the wrath of his comrades. What did come as a surprise was the violence with which they were committed to their politics. Papa was declared a "class enemy" in no time.

It was a denunciation that didn't bode well for him. Luckily, he escaped from the clutches of his vengeful ex-comrades. It wasn't luck that saved him though. A close friend with considerable influence intervened in the nick of time. He persuaded the hot-headed communists to abandon their plans to attack my father for the crime of expressing his dissent plainly. Papa obviously had the right to speak his mind. He could obviously dissociate himself from an ideology he had once enthusiastically endorsed but had understandably begun to loathe. As it turned out, it wasn't obvious at all. That cast the ideology and its proponents in a decisively poor light.

He shared this experience when she was in her early 30s. She listened to him with rapt attention, discovering something new about her father's life history. If there was anything she could ever be sure of, it was her dad's ability to amaze her even after so many years of sharing a special bond, which was forged the day she was born and strengthened as she grew up and developed a way of thinking distinctly her own. As long as he lived, he enriched and enraptured her with the vastness of his knowledge, the rarity of his common sense, the fascinating anecdotes he pulled out from his repertoire of life experience, and the spectacularly correct predictions he made with his preternatural vision. He was no soothsayer, nor did he care about soothsayers. He was a man of science who seemed to possess an intuition developed with experience and knowledge. But that couldn't explain everything about him. He carried within him some magic that made him miraculously talented. He was great. And he was gone.

5

A Bumpy Ride on a Starry Night

It was 2am. Reena had been assigned the late-night shift. The company driver was tardy as usual. After a long wait came the creaking sound of a cab. Reena watched the vehicle moving drunkenly, as if it had guzzled alcohol instead of petrol. It belched out nauseating fumes that assailed her from afar. She groaned at the thought of travelling in this vehicle, but she had no option. This was the cab assigned to her today and no other cab was in sight at the moment. Besides, there were others waiting for their cabs, scanning their surroundings with eagle eyes lest some jerk outsmart them and get into the vehicle out of turn.

There was a scarcity of cabs today, which was the case every day. So, there was no scope for choosing your cab. You were supposed to be grateful if the cab assigned to you arrived, even if its condition made it seem like you were going to have the last ride of your life.

The cab stopped near her. It was in a ramshackle state and crying out for repair. Reena felt that the car was past the stage of repair and renewal. It actually had no business being on the roads. But then, the other cabs were scarcely more appealing: just a shade better, which could only be discerned if you looked at the cabs very closely.

The company cabs reminded you of frail senior citizens tottering while getting to their destination. The cabs shook and rattled as they moved, keeping you on tenterhooks till you reached your destination. Minor accidents were fairly common and treated with superb casualness. You never knew when a cab would screech to a halt on the middle of the road because of some malfunction that could very well turn out to be unfixable. So, you were stranded on a road with fast-moving traffic. Quite often, you sat on the divider if it was not crammed with plants or swathed with bougainvillea that left no room for you to fit in. In that case, you had no option but to stick closely to the divider while cars and motorcycles within touching distance zipped past you. There were autorickshaws that moved pell-mell, threatening to ram into you. Getting home should not have been such a herculean task, but, unfortunately, it was. The ride home was full of terrors besides being time-consuming and uncomfortable—the cushion on the back seat would have frayed so much that it was like a wooden seat; the windows would either not open or refuse to close; some doors couldn't even be locked and clattered as the car moved, compelling you to squeeze close to the passenger next you, lest the door opened and threw you on the road.

Reena opened the door and sat inside the cab, a lone passenger (no one was going in that direction) trembling with a sense of foreboding. "God, get me home safely. I have been so good today. And you know I do my best every day. That must earn me the right to live. Keep me safe," she appealed to God with her hands joined in the form of a prayer.

Reena couldn't tell if this dilapidated cab was falling into disrepair or if it had already outlived its utility. Whatever stage of decay the cab was in, it was definitely not fit to be driven on roads even if it could be forced to operate longer than it was advisable. A ride in this cab could very well shorten Reena's lifespan, given the deadly mix of rash driving, roads riddled with potholes, and an aged engine that could announce retirement anytime. If that wasn't frightening enough, drunk drivers would weave madly through vehicles. What scared Reena the most was the mushrooming of reckless bikers who laid claim to the road at this late hour and zoomed past you one after another at a speed befitting a race: a dangerous race to some finishing line that was likely to finish someone or the other in a collision waiting to happen.

Whenever she was travelling in the company car, Reena would keep her eyes wide open to spot danger from a distance lest the driver dozed off or didn't slow down in time—a strong possibility given the fatigue caused by working overtime and the tearing hurry to finish one trip, so that more employees could be dropped to their destination and the total number of trips could ensure sufficient earnings for the day.

Reena was in a contemplative mood today, unlike most days when she was too exhausted to think. She adjusted herself to find the most comfortable posture. She looked out of the window and gazed at the sky, which was dotted with more stars than she had seen in a long time. The shimmer in the sky accentuated the dinginess of the cab. She worked for no small company but their cabs testified to its stinginess. It was amazing how employers flush with money could be so tight-fisted. Their miserliness presented them in a pathetic light. The employees loved to hate the company. Reena was indifferent to it. She was not the one to fritter away her emotions on anyone or anything not worth thinking about. She had to make a living, so she had no option but to agree for car rides fraught with danger. And the company that had hired her was blissfully unconcerned about her safety, who, like every other employee, was disposable. Maybe that's why they made all the arrangements to literally dispose her off. Something caught her eye all of a sudden. The handle for opening the door was hanging loose and would have come off if she wasn't careful. She looked at the handle closely and felt like it was an inanimate replica of her. On most days she was stretched to a point that she would come part if put under further strain. The handle too was incapable of withstanding any strain; it had been pulled too roughly and too often. Everything was stretched to breaking point in this wretched company that loved to flaunt its achievements and refused to acknowledge its failings, sweeping under the rug every one of them, as if this was their official policy. Well, it might very well be. It was definitely their unofficial policy—known to everyone but accepted without much protest. People needed a job. So, they had to endure exploitation without making a complaint or calling things by their name.

Reena had made peace with this awful state of affairs. And although her day was as tiring as ever, a sense of calm pervaded her being. The driver started the car, which produced a great deal of noise conveying its reluctance to be pushed any further. It took a few moments before the car started with a jerk. Reena flew off her seat and hit her forehead on the headrest of the seat in front. An ominous start to a perilous journey. She massaged her forehead throbbing with pain and instructed the driver to better be careful. The car lurched a few times before it began to run smoothly, i.e., as smoothly as a decrepit vehicle could run.

Reena looked out of the window, noticing nothing in particular but taking in everything she saw. The driver, a burly man with a booming voice that could easily drown out the grating sound produced incessantly by the rundown car, was accompanied by a skinny guard meant to ensure the safety a female employee.

Reena didn't wish to dwell upon the guard's appearance lest her scrutinizing gaze caught his attention and made him self-conscious. Even so, a thought flitted through her mind. He was a gaunt fellow who couldn't possibly contend with the well-fed driver if anything untoward happened. If things came to blows, the guard would be overpowered with great ease. The emaciated fellow was in need of protection himself. The tall and well-built driver could lift them both at once and throw them headfirst on the road, if he got possessed by rage or the devil incarnate.

The car kept bouncing and tilting left and right as it traversed potholed roads. The driver, imposing by temperament, blew the horn incessantly, scaring vehicles out of his way without slowing his pace even once. He drove like he was an emperor who naturally expected vehicles to clear the way for him on seeing him approach. Suddenly, he started prattling, "What's the point of paying one's salary when you've managed to tide over the difficult times. When you're famished, you'll value food but after you've managed to benefactor who has supplied you with all your needs, you won't even care for a sumptuous *thali*, especially if it is served by the misers who withheld your dues. Poverty compels you to suffer in silence and work for people you would rather spit at," he said with fervour edged with resentment.

He was obviously pained, struggling to feed his family, but the ease with which he held conversations did not bear a hint of his suffering.

The car continued to wobble even on smooth roads with hardly any traffic. The only respite was that it shook less, and that was the best you could expect from a vehicle that seemed on the verge of falling to pieces. Reena saw scores of homeless people sleeping on the pavement. Some shivered in the cold; some covered themselves with a tattered blanket; some generated warmth by clinging to each other, taking turns to chafe each other's hands and feet. Women clasped their children to the bosom and covered them with a saree. Some men seem too drunk to lift a finger and lay sprawled wherever they had apparently dropped. Men with tangled hair and grimy faces slept soundly. There was dignity in their quiet acceptance of deprivation. They were as human as those ensconced in their beds in palatial houses. They were as susceptible to pain, as desirous of comfort, as conscious of their unjust living conditions, as frustrated with penury, as resentful of deep inequality, as anyone in their position would be. No one gets used to privation and scarcity, but one perseveres in the worst of circumstances. What option does one have?

Travelling through Delhi's roads always pained Reena. So many people passed by the homeless and penniless without so much as batting an eyelid. What made these people so insensitive? Did they attribute the wretched state of their fellow humans to karma? Did they consider their poverty to be a part of God's grand design. Maybe they expected him to dole out benefits and blessings selectively, depending on whom He deemed worthy. He couldn't equally bestow favours upon everybody, they must have argued with themselves. Even if there was suffering, He would have a reason for it. Things couldn't be so arbitrary when God was watching over everything. And so, the luckier mortals benumbed their conscience and got on with their lives with perfect equanimity, even if they were surrounded by immeasurable misery.

Reena turned her gaze away from the window. It was too painful to see unmitigated suffering treated with easy indifference or dismissed before sympathy was awakened for the suffering multitudes. She counted her blessings and prayed for the masses relegated to the margins of society. She closed her eyes as she said a long prayer to lessen her guilt at her inability to do much for those in dire straits and terrible need for help. She went into a trance while praying which was rudely broken when the car swerved sharply to prevent a head-on collision with a vehicle coming from the wrong side at break-neck speed. The collision was averted but the car rammed into the divider. The occupants of the car were dislodged from their seats and lunged forward with great force. First, Reena slipped from her seat and fell on the flooring of the car. When she tried to get up, she was again propelled forward and banged her head against the back of the front passenger seat. Before she could hold on to something to prevent further damage, the car rammed into the divider and was temporarily lifted off the ground. Reena, who was raising herself from the flooring, was hurled upwards by the violent movements of the sharply veering and forcefully crashing vehicle. Her head slammed against the roof of the car. She was expecting to be buffeted left and right for quite some time with the bruises piling up and perhaps even a bone breaking with the impact of the mishap. But the jerky movements stopped and the car was perfectly still. For a while, there was the silence of the graveyard. Everyone was in too much pain to analyse what just transpired. In this antiquated specimen of a car, there were hardly any safeguards. No seatbelt on the backseat. Damaged seatbelts on the front. No airbag for rescue. The handles meant to minimize the shock of a jerk was all broken except one. Even the handle of the car door to be pulled for getting out was ready to fall off anytime. Reena turned her gaze towards and saw that the door handle had indeed become detached from the door. When the pain began to subside, Reena said to the driver, "Please call the company and request for another cab. I, for the life of me, won't travel with you anymore." The driver gave her a mulish look, making it clear that he would drag this wreck of a car till the destination. To temper the effect of his look, he said, "The car hasn't been damaged so much. I save us from a collision. It's not my fault if some drunken fellow drives in the opposite direction instead of taking the adjacent road assigned for traffic going that way. My car is in tip-top condition. It can absorb such shocks and run like a horse." Though there was truth in what the driver said, Reena got out of the car and started searching for an autorickshaw or some decent-looking driver that might offer her a lift. The driver called her back many times, but she had had enough.

Reena walked away in a huff. The driver's voice grated in her ears. As she kept moving ahead, the sound grew faint till it could be heard no more. Something deep inside made her stop for a moment and gaze at the star-lit sky, which shone more brightly than before. Even in the thick of the night, when darkness reigned supreme, the stars served as a beacon of hope by shining a light. Reena realized that things wouldn't be so hopeless if you didn't resign yourself to daily oppression. You had to find the light even if darkness seemed to hold sway. The light was still there. When the sun spread its glorious beams, everything was awash with light: all was clear and distinct. A feeling of calmness washed over her. She was done with her wretched job. Better things awaited her. She hailed an auto that seemed to materialize just in time. She got in and negotiated a fair price. As the auto headed in the direction of her home, she thanked God for being alive. She reached her place sooner than expected. As she stepped out of the autorickshaw, she glanced one last time at the star-bedecked sky. "So beautiful!" she exclaimed. A smile lit up her face. As she entered her house, equally beautiful hopes bloomed inside her heart.

Acknowledgments

A special thanks to:

My dear brother, Vaibhav, who knows the true meaning of unconditional love and bestows it on me very generously.

My manager, Mr Mukesh, who came like a godlike figure when I was in the depths of despair.

My good old friend Parakram, who has been there for me through happy times and rainy days.

Dheeraj, whose brilliant housekeeping saves from the tedium of domestic chores. I can't think of a greater blessing.

Mama, my deep love for you cannot be force-fitted into words.

Papa, I miss you. Ever since you left your earthly abode, a part of you seems to live in me and through me. It seems like our voices have merged into a miraculous medley of biting wit, scathing sarcasm, throbbing emotions and poignant reflections. It's hard to know where you begin and I end. You may be gone, and yet you are always here with me in spirit. I hope it stays this way as long as I live.